T0193983

A THANKYA DON'T COST YA' NOTHIN'

T BROOKS

WESTBOW
PRESS®
A DIVISION OF THOMAS NELSON
& ZONDERVAN

THE HOLY BIBLE, NEW INTERNATIONAL VERSION®,
NIV® Copyright © 1973, 1978, 1984, 2011 by Biblica, Inc.®
Used by permission. All rights reserved worldwide.

Scripture taken from the NEW AMERICAN STANDARD BIBLE®,
Copyright © 1960, 1962, 1963, 1968, 1971, 1972, 1973, 1975, 1977,
1995 by The Lockman Foundation. Used by permission."

Scripture taken from the King James Version of the Bible.

The Authorized (King James) Version of the Bible ('the KJV'), the
rights in which are vested in the Crown in the United Kingdom, is
reproduced here by permission of the Crown's patentee, Cambridge
University Press. The Cambridge KJV text including paragraphing, is
reproduced here by permission of Cambridge University Press.

This is a work of fiction. All of the characters, names, incidents,
organizations, and dialogue in this novel are either the products
of the author's imagination or are used fictitiously.

WestBow Press books may be ordered through booksellers or by contacting:

WestBow Press
A Division of Thomas Nelson & Zondervan
1663 Liberty Drive
Bloomington, IN 47403
www.westbowpress.com
1 (866) 928-1240

Because of the dynamic nature of the Internet, any web addresses or
links contained in this book may have changed since publication and
may no longer be valid. The views expressed in this work are solely those
of the author and do not necessarily reflect the views of the publisher,
and the publisher hereby disclaims any responsibility for them.

Any people depicted in stock imagery provided by Getty Images are models,
and such images are being used for illustrative purposes only.
Certain stock imagery © Getty Images.

ISBN: 978-1-9736-2043-3 (sc)
ISBN: 978-1-9736-2042-6 (e)

Library of Congress Control Number: 2018902112

Print information available on the last page.

WestBow Press rev. date: 02/22/2018

ACKNOWLEDGEMENTS

To God Be The Glory For The Things He Has Done

The saints say to understand my praise, you first must know my story (cue the music) that's a teaser for the next book

I must thank God for the gift of writing and creativity that lay waiting to be cultivated and brought forth in me.

A very special thank you to my publicist Rita Moore for all her support in seeing in me what I didn't see myself. She took notice of my gift and helped me to bring it to fruition.

Thank you to Helen Morris and Morris Moments Photography for making me look so naturally beautiful.

Thank you to John Morris and ForeverYoung &Co for my fabulous custom shirt.

This being my first book, I have many people to include in this wonderful moment, please bear with me. I promise the second book won't be as long, lol.

Thank you to the best Sunday School Supertendent in the world Deacon Jason Perry for allowing God to use you one Sunday morning and testify one morning setting the house on fiyaa!

This book is dedicated to my father Episcopal Deacon John Pradia Jr. If he was here today he were here today, he would smile and say, "that girl did it!'

To my mother, Bishop Helen Pradia and the Praise Temple Apostolic Church thank you for laying hands on me at a young age and praying for me and if you are ever in the Greater Houston Area stops by the Hot Spot!! Baby Praise Temple takes it to Church over there!

My Children Helen, John(LaToya) and Patrick(Jessica) You are the children a parent wished they had and I'm honored to be your mom!

Zoey, John Jr, Mason, Zion, Heaven, Josiah, Mariah, Neveah, Isiah, and Olivia
Grandma Luv U

My sisters Aretha and Schavon, brothers James, Lenny, Jermaine and Michael
Big Sis Loves You!

To my Mother-In-Love Mary Brooks thank you for being there you have been such a wall of support.
I love you

My Sisters-in-love Michelle, Willie Mae and
my Brothers-in-love Mark(Dean)and King
Thank you for loving me. I love you

My, Sweet Peas Shara, Eshakay, Candice and
Mitoya, the best god daughters this side of heaven.
Thank you for keeping your god mother
young with this new language lol

To Supertendent and Lady Tisdell and the
New Bethel Temple COGIC family thank
you for all of your support and prayers!

My Spiritual Mom Curlie Simmons Thank
You For your hugs and talks Love you!

My Prayer Sisters Dr. Tina Williams, Missionary
Clara Carrington, Sis. Cindi Thomas, Hugs

To my Cali family I love you!! There is an old song that say God has a way of doing things and I like the way he does it. Some years ago, God began to mend a relationship between my biological father and myself. I didn't forget to put him in the beginning of my acknowledgments, I saved this until the end because it was something I really wanted someone to read. God will mend and repair at a time when the tear is great, and you feel its unmendable. I lost my step father who raised me in 2013 and I'm a daddy's girl so my heart felt unmendable. I'm grateful for the relationship he and I share today with my dad, and it gets stronger each day. I love you Dad and Celia

My Austrian Shephard Sadie, Supreme
Doggie Snacks baby!!

To My Darling Husband Richard, we have been through Hurricane Ike, the Memorial Day Floods 2 and then my pacemaker surgery in July and Hurricane Harvey August losing everything we own in the flood, but we held to each other and our faith in God. We will continue to hold to the promised of God and move forward
I Love You

FOREWORD

A Thankya Don't Cost Ya Nothin' came from a testimony given on a Sunday morning. God deserves our Thankya! At times we go about our daily lives like he owes us the air we breathe.

Well….

The next time blessing come your way, or grace and mercy protect you from danger and its arms around you like a blanket on a cold winter night remember….

A Thankya Don't Cost Ya Nothin"

CHAPTER

ONE

The musicians were on Fiyaa this morning!!!
Everyone was on their feet clapping, singing,
waving their hands and giving God due praise.

The praise and worship team were singing so hard
I thought the Angels were going to come down
and take them to heaven. I looked around the
sanctuary and smiled. I loved my church. I had been
a member for a few years and yes, most churches
had its issues, but I really loved my church.

As the music got quiet and worship ended one
of the Deacons stood to testify. Every church has
that Deacon that is the coolest, best dressed, well
versed deacon in the church that minds his own
business but knows yours without you knowing it?

Deacon Chill stood and began to tell of the goodness
of God. The music trilled in the background and
the mothers began to say well son speak the word!
Deac went on to say how as he got older and acquired
more in life he got more Thankful and a tear rolled
down his face. Somebody jumped up and said
yes lawd and someone else ran down the aisle.

Deac said if you don't remember anything
in this lifetime always remember that

A Thankya Don't Cost You Nothin'!

I felt a cold chill down my spine and looked
over at my husband who was praising God.

My stomach was growling, and I had a huge
presentation to present to the partners tomorrow. I
loved my church, but I really hoped Pastor didn't
hoop too long today. I have a big day tomorrow
that may lead to a whole new tax bracket for me.

Once the musicians lowered the music and the
pastor got up to speak with a loud voice She said
Lift those sanctified hands and tell God Thankya!
She was a little woman in stature but when the
anointing took over you were in awe and when she
sung, her voice was so sweet it brought tears to your
eyes. The saints began to worship, and Bishop raised
her hands and said okay, lets get our bibles and go
to the word of the Lord and see what is says:

Colossians 3:15 And let the peace of God rule in your
hearts, to the which also ye are called in one body: and
be ye thankful (KJV)

CHAPTER

TWO

Baby! Are you going to church today? No, I have a proposal I'm working on and I won't make it.

My husband looked at me as if I just told him the world was ending. "You haven't been to church in months!

The bible says in Hebrews 10:25 - Not forsaking the assembling of ourselves together, as the manner of some [is]; but exhorting [one another]: and so much the more, as ye see the day approaching." (AKJV)

My husband shook his head in disappointment. I heard him go upstairs and say a quick prayer.

Lord, you have given us everything we desired. Beautiful home, successful careers, several cars and more finances than we really know what to do with.

My wife has forgotten. Please God, Bring her back.

Thankya In Advance

Your Servant Steven

Steven walked down the stairs with a heavy heart but smiled when he saw his wife sitting on the chaise sipping a latte. He loved the air this woman breathed. She was his rib. He bent he huge frame down to kiss her and told her he would meet her for lunch after service. Next Sunday Veronica? She kept looking at TV and smiled that patronizing smile.

Tell everyone hello for me I said as I looked at my handsome husband. He was wearing that suit and the cologne was tickling my senses making me want to give him a reason to stay home this morning and say hallelujah….

I couldn't remember the last time I had been to church and to tell you the truth I didn't really miss it, my friends, yes but the politics of "church" no I didn't miss it at all.

With TV evangelist and social media and online music who really needed to step into the church doors anymore?

I just watch a preacher on social media, listen to a little music and send in a financial donation to the ministry of my choice. Spiritual experience taken care of, yes, I'm good.

My career is on point and I just made partner at Burke Lyles & Dukes, the largest Accounting Firm in the Greater Houston area.

Some may say I'm proud or boastful but I'm on way and I don't need the old-time church folk making me feel bad for making it. So, I just stay away.

My husband Steven is more into it than me, so I let him do us if that makes sense.

Well enough of me daydreaming, not going to get any work done today, might as well hit the spa since everyone is at church today.

I love Sundays, shopping, brunch, spa, then a quick nap while honey is at church. A nice dinner prepared by Chef since I called him on his day off today… Hey I don't like to cook.

Love my life….

Little did I know I was going to need to open the doors of the church sooner than I thought.

CHAPTER

THREE

Veronica strutted into the offices of Burke Lyles & Duke with the air of royalty. Her hair, nails and outfit were on fleek and she knew she was representing Whitney Houston's song Every Woman this morning.

Beth, please get my usual coffee, bagel and messages and this time don't let me have to ask for apple slices with my bagel. Beth sighed and smiled into the phone "yes maam."

Veronica walked away from the intercom, shaking her head and picked up her morning files, good help is so hard to find. Beth went to her husband's church and at Steven's request gave her this job, but she is one mistake from being fired.

Yes, I am hard to work for, but perfection takes work and if you can't take it walk away.

Did I walk away from you? Came a soft voice? I looked around seeing no-one.

Beth is always quoting Matthew 7:12 Therefore all things whatsoever ye would that men should do to you, do ye even so to them: for this is the law and the prophets. (KJV)

She remembers the scriptures well but always forgets my sliced apples or getting my dry cleaning. Most people say I'm hard on her, but she is so easy. It's all about church. No social life.

I sat down to look at a few accounts that were heavy hitters. I was told to give them special attention and well I didn't give them my best but hey being in my presence should have been the icing on the cake for them. The latest account I canceled on and sent them a beautiful gift basket and had their financials airmailed it to them. When I called, them they said they would email me their response after looking over my proposal and numbers.

That was my hair appointment day and I would not keep Rey Rey waiting cause honey she knows how to beat this hair, so the gift basket and airmail of the financials and numbers where excellent customer care in Veronica's eyes.

Veronica got up to go to the ladies' room and heard Beth in the stall next to hers. She heard her talking to someone and smirked to herself, so Beth isn't so sweet after all.

I don't know how much more I can take Beth was saying. She taunts me all day. She makes fun of my clothing and I do work that isn't related to my job description. I'm thankful for the job but I can't take much more. Thank you for all you do for me and I love you Jesus Amen.

Veronica Felt like a ball had hit her in the stomach. Did I really do these things? Was I really this bad? This is business and its only business, she tried to make herself feel better for her disrespectful actions towards her employee. Maybe Beth needs to work in another field Veronica thought as she again tried to clear her conscience.

She waited until she heard the stall door close and water running and the outside door close letting her know Beth had exited before she quietly left out.

While thinking about firing her 4[Th] receptionist in the 3months since being made partner, the red line buzzed on her desk. Veronica looked at the phone thinking that's strange why didn't Beth let me know I was getting a call dispatched through to the red line. The Phone rang again and yet again Beth didn't answer, Veronica mused, maybe Beth decided to go back to the restroom and say a word of prayer, well she is going to need it when I get off this call. No bagel, no coffee and now the red line rings and I get no heads up. Veronica let it ring 1 more time before answering, Veronica Neal how may I help you?

Veronica you are wanted in the red room immediately!!

CHAPTER

FOUR

Veronica stared at the phone and heard the dial tone. No other words were needed. The red room was where deals made. She was made partner in the red room, deals were broken, people fired, and dreams made and broken in the red room.

Veronica began to smile and got up to dance a jig!!! In her mind only the positive could happen to her because she is the best at what she does. This must be a huge account and want only the best on it. There had been talk of merging of accounts, so she figured she is probably getting the larger accounts.

Veronica smiled and saw herself driving the new 2017 Jaguar XJ in a sleek silver with black interior fully loaded with all the bells and whistles. She would have to sweeten the pot with Steven because he was upset when she came home with her last baby, a 2016 Hummer H3 with her name in the head rest. A girl needs cars like she needs shoes.

She already saw herself driving that new vehicle and saw taking trips, experiencing new mud spa locations in Europe and more.

Where is my coffee!!! This is huge, and I need my coffee and bagel before I go into this meeting. I don't want my stomach growling making me look hungry and foolish.

Lord help me this girl is so fired when I leave this meeting.

Smile girl, go do yo thang Veronica thought as she power strutted towards the Red Room

I walked into the Red Room as it was called due to all the power plays, careers that had been catapulted to media status, blood sweat and tears that went into the work and success that each and every employee endured which made and was in this very room thus giving it the name

The Red Room.

I was the only female ever to make partner and took advantage of letting everyone knowing it every chance I got. I was special, a rare gem that they should be happy and grateful to have yet they didn't act like it. I will have to show them. These clients should be happy I work for them, but they complain and complain all the time. Makes me want a massage. Oooh that sounds good right now. Veronica had to reign her thoughts in, what where they saying? Not happy with her performance, customers complaining? Hold on... Bret the Human Resource Manager was talking, when had he gotten there, or had he been at the table the whole time?

Veronica we're sorry but on all 3 accounts they have decided to take their business to another firm. They feel that we just don't care about them. That isn't how we do business and not how we have done business. We did not get to be the top firm in Houston by skimping on customer service.

Your credit statements show you have had spa visits, dinners and recently purchased a Hummer H3.

We did tell you to spend lavishly on our clients and make them feel like royalty, but it seems like you have mistaken the meaning of what we told you to do most of these charges placed on the company card are done after business hours or when we contact our client's sectary to send them a follow up gift basket which is our procedure after partners have wined and dined them, they have notified them they have not met with you. You have either canceled or sent them fruit baskets. We don't send fruit baskets.... We are a multimillion dollar company. Our follow up baskets costs no less than $10,000 We send clients spa packages, sport event tickets and more.

We are going to send you home and let you think and evaluate if you want to really want to be a part of this firm or not and we are going to evaluate if you are really a fit for Burke Lyle & Duke.

We will see you in a couple of weeks. Your clientele will be given to another partner to handle. We will need all your credit cards, passcodes, and the keys to the vehicle as you exit the building today.

"How am I to get home I drove this morning" Veronica asked.

That isn't for us to worry about. We are to salvage your accounts. Also, you will be off without pay. With that everyone rose from table leaving Veronica sitting at the table in the red room crying feeling as if she had just lost the golden chalet.

How was she going to explain this to Steven? They were in so much debt due to her overspending and he didn't know it. She had just accepted this job but as soon as she signed the papers, she also signed one the house, cars, jewels and more.

Keeping up with the Joneses? They were the Joneses she would brag her inner circle!

Lord what have I done?

Veronica sat for a while longer and heard a soft whisper in her ear

When pride comes, then comes disgrace, but with humility comes wisdom. Proverbs 11:2 (NIV)

Veronica shook it off thinking she was just stressing of how to tell Steven she had been temporarily laid off or something. Maybe a nice dinner one that I will cook myself not chef and a little romance. Yes, food and intimacy with a good movie, he will be okay and not notice I will still be in the bed when he leaves for work in the morning. That's what I'll will do Veronica thought. Dinner, romance and a movie and he will be putty in her hands. Well now to walk this hall of shame to my office and transfer these files, turn in my keys and surrender my things until I get back Veronica was thinking.

This is only temporary, they need me. I'll probably get a call before I make it home today. Now to think of a place to put these boxes of my things as not to make Steven suspicious she thought. Veronica was so into her thoughts she didn't see her secretary in the human resource office, and she was singing like a bird, thanks to the nice incentive she was just was given.

CHAPTER

FIVE

"Honey, I'm home" Veronica called from the front door as she brought in Stevens favorite takeout. She knew Steven would not be home yet but just in case he was she had her things sent to her frat sister Dominique's home because she would keep her secret until she could tell Steven or, so she thought.

Girl, Mz thang got sent home! Dominique was telling someone on the phone. I know right, she supposed to be so good, but she was over here crying and snottin and saying please don't tell nobody. I guess she forgot how she did me when I was needin a ride and my baby was sick and had to catch the bus. The lady she was talking to didn't say anything but kept quiet and listened on the phone.

Dominique said did you hear what I was saying, Mz high and mighty done fell isn't that great? Kiesha said "Dominique why are acting like that, we should pray for her, lets pray now, I will pray, and you can just listen-

Dear Lord, we ask that you touch Veronica and fix this situation that she and her husband Steven are enduring at this moment."

Dominique interrupted and said "Kiesha I must go, I have someone else to call, you go ahead and pray, talk to you later" as she laughed hanging up the phone.

Kiesha felt trouble in the air and started praying and interceding for her friend. She began to call out the spirit of confusion. While praying the scripture came to her

1 Corinthians 14:33 For God is not the author of confusion, but of **peace**, as in all churches of the saints(KJV)

Keisha cried out in prayer for Veronica and Steven and Psalms 91 dropped in her spirit:

Heavenly Father, I ask You to place a hedge of protection around my friends. To hide them from the enemy and all demon spirits making it difficult, if not impossible for them to effectively track or trace them in the realm of the spirit. There shall be no perforations or penetrations to these hedges of protection according to your word in Psalm 91. I know that You will answer this prayer because I love You and I trust in Your name only. I pray that Your Blood Lord Jesus will cover them and all that You have given them.

Thankya in advance for their victory!

Keisha began to praise God in her living room for Veronica and Steven.

She knew God had it all in control and couldn't wait to put a praise on it with the couple.

Keisha began to load her dishwasher, thinking to herself, being single has its perks. I can come home from work, hit the gym, and after a light dinner, get in my word without having to worry about a husband to answer to.

While being single had its perks, Keisha desired a husband. Her father also her pastor Bishop Lemon said it's all about what you do while you wait. So, Keisha worked with the singles ministry while she waited. She also worked with the youth. Being the singles ministry leader kept Keisha busy and she was loving ministry. Shut in prayer was her favorite because it afforded her the luxury of being able to lay out before God and just pray. Communing and talking to the Lord, reading her bible and helping young women. This Saturday the women of the ministry were going to visit the local shelter and pass out toiletries and care packs. This is what mission is about. Ministry filled her void but deep down she knew ministry couldn't fill some voids or needs. Lord, I'm waiting on you, but can you please hurry, I'm not getting any younger.

One morning while gathering the supplies to take to the mission Keisha's mother asked her when was she going to start looking for a husband. Keisha, you aren't getting any younger. Pretty soon you are going to be too old to give me and your father grandchildren.

Keisha gave her the look she gives the kids in children church and said Mother, the bible says:

in **Proverbs 18:22** that *He* who finds a *wife* finds a *good* thing…. (NIV)

Before Keisha could finish her scripture, her mother raised her hands on her hips and said fine! Her mother put her hand on her hip and said how you think I got your daddy? Honey, I believe in prayer but when he saw me he was the one praying. She then kissed Keisha on the cheek and said I'll see you over there.

Bishop Lemon walked over to his only child and gave her a big bear hug. He shook his head and laughed at his wife's antics.

Keisha was a daddy's girl and talked to her daddy about any and everything spiritual as well as natural. She wanted to take the focus from herself and marriage and talk about her friends Veronica and Steven who were also close family friends of Bishops as well.

Bishop wouldn't let the subject go this time and he had a determined look in his eyes.

Key, his name for her since she was a little girl, we just want you to be happy. We want you to experience everything life must offer. You have traveled this world from one end to the other. You have done everything and conquered all you set out to do. I know you desire a husband because you spoke this to me. I pray as a father that God gives you the desires of your heart.

Meanwhile...

CHAPTER

SIX

What were you thinking? Did you think I wouldn't find out you got fired? Unbelievable! Here I am thinking I am at fault pushing you too hard about going to church with me during the week and on Sundays and you have been lying to me the whole time!

The trips, excursions and expensive reservations to dinner were they on the company card? Say something, don't just sit there not saying anything.

Veronica sat in silence looking like she had seen a ghost. She had just walked in from spending a beautiful morning getting a massage then taking advantage of a private dress sale at Barneys by a private distributor. How had he known that fast the company had called and told her they had chosen to go in another direction and would not renew her contract. They sent her a courier with her final contract amended with 6-month salary and paid benefits.

Veronica looked at the phone after the call ended and her door bell rung. The courier service was at the door which meant they were probably outside when she came in, but she was so excited about her purchases she didn't see him.

Veronica's heart fell and beat fast in her chest. Lord how will she tell Steven she was let go from the very job she just started less than 2 years ago? Steven was thinking that she was just let go but wait until he finds out that she has been off for a while now. Veronica's mind began to wander, and she began to think back… Steven begged Veronica to stay at her last job because she had stability and the partner position was passed around in the ears of the right people, but Veronica couldn't wait. She felt that her being a woman in an arena of men would hinder her from getting the attention she needed to secure the position of partner. Steven told her all she had to do was pray and begin to thank God for the position in advance and walk in it, but Veronica said it took more than that.

Steven quoted Mark 11:24 -Therefore I tell you, whatever you ask for in prayer, believe that you have received it, and it will be yours (NIV)

Veronica switched out of the room shaking her head with frustration saying Steven please, stop already doesn't the bible say if you make one step he'll make two? With a coy smile on her face. Steven walked up behind veronica and said What? Woman don't you play with Gods words! When it came to the bible Steven was kingdom minded. He played no games at all.

Veronica brought her mind back to the present, Steven was still going on and now he was quoting scripture something about being ungrateful for the job and how so many people would be happy for the opportunities we have. Veronica was getting ready to speak when the doorbell rang. Saved by the bell, or so she thought.

CHAPTER

SEVEN

Steven went to answer the door and you could have bought Veronica for half a cent when the door swung opened.

Dominique came in like a cold wind with her arms full saying there are boxes downstairs that need to be brought up. Steven looked on confused, hello to you Dom. What's going on? He was used to Dominique having drama in her life. Dominique came in dramatic and dropped the boxes on the living room floor. Hey Steven! Talking loudly, I'm sorry to hear about my frat sissy's firing last week, but I can't keep these boxes at my place any longer, I just don't have the space for them. Veronica could have fallen through the floor but unfortunately no such luck today. She stood there waiting for the rapture or any crazy wild act of nature to happen. Where are those things you see on tv, people getting wings and flying away, people disappearing, holes swallowing people up, Veronica looked around her and closed her eyes for a second and reopened them. If I twitch my nose like I dream of Jeanie will I disappear? She twitched and nothing.

Lawd, if I ever needed you I need you now….

Dominique left Steven and Veronica's home thinking she had done major damage. She let the devil use her and she figured she had caused not only dissension in the home, but she showed Steven that she was more woman than Veronica will ever be. What kind of woman gets fired and doesn't tell her husband but hides the evidence at another woman's house.

My mama always said if you lie you'll steal, if you steal you'll kill. I don't know if it applies to her getting fired or not but right now it sounds right to me. Ooweee, the look her face when I walked in all innocent with those boxes. I knew Steven didn't know that gal had gotten fired. People always think I'm slow, but they don't know I'm just on time. Dominique got back in her car and drove down the street. She was still talking to herself driving, I wonder what lie she is coming up with now. Can't lie your way out of this one little Mrs "We Are The Jones"

Yea, I Showed Mz Thang!

Dominique called Kiesha to tell her what she had done but got her voicemail. She left a message laughing hysterically as she drove erratically across the lanes on the street. Dominique kept trying to find a station on the radio but didn't find a song to fit her mood. She cut the radio off and sped down the street.

Her phone rang, and it was Kiesha. Dominique began to tell her what she did but Kiesha stopped her and said Dominique, I want to pray for you right now. I am feeling something in my spirit and its troubling me. Danger is coming.

Dominique laughed and said save your prayers I'm fine and disconnected the call and threw the phone on the seat next to her just as Kiesha began to pray for her friend's safety and her mental state.

Kiesha prayed anyway: Lord, please watch over Dominique and protect her mentally. The sprit of jealousy we bind now in the name of Jesus and the bible states that in Job 5:2 "For anger slays the foolish man, and jealousy kills the simple (NAS)

We bind this spirit at the root and we ask you to loose Dominique in the mighty name of Jesus Christ!

Kiesha began to speak in heavenly tongues and intercede on her friend's behalf. God your will be done regarding Dominique. Thankya in advance for her testimony!

CHAPTER

EIGHT

To Dominique she had done the right thing. Reaching for her cell on the seat next to her Dominique thought she heard a voice soft in her ear saying Dominique one day we will all have to atone for our sins, we all are not perfect, my word says *in Romans 3:23: For all have sinned and fall short of the glory of God (NIV)*

Speeding down the street Dominique began to cry, God I just wanted Veronica to hurt, wanted her to feel my pain. She had it all good job, husband, home. God I'm sorry. Wiping Tears and her ringing phone she wasn't paying attention to the road. NO

Looking at her phone it was Veronica, she answered but before she gets out hello Veronica screamed "What Were You Thinking?" and Dominique never got the chance to answer because she didn't see the 18wheeler careening from her passenger side as she ran the red light.

All Veronica heard was metal and glass exploding like a loud boom!

Veronica looks at the phone Dom Dom are you there ?!?.... Hello???? No!!!!

Want to See What Happens Next?

Tune in for A Thankya Don't Cost Ya Nothin' 2

You don't want to miss what happens in the life of these 3 lifelong friends Veronica, Dominque and Kiesha as they realize A Thankya Don't Cost Ya Nothin

Printed in the United States
By Bookmasters